The Ugly Duckling

The Ugly Duckling

by Hans Christian Andersen

Translated by R. P. Keigwin

Illustrated by Adrienne Adams

Charles Scribner's Sons • New York

Summertime! How lovely it was out in the country, with the wheat standing yellow, the oats green, and the hay all stacked down in the grassy meadows! And there went the stork on his long red legs, chattering away in Egyptian, for he had learnt that language from his mother. The fields and meadows had large woods all around, and in the middle of the woods there were deep lakes.

Yes, it certainly was lovely out in the country. Bathed in sunshine stood an old manor house with a deep moat round it, and growing out of the wall down by the water were huge dock-leaves; the biggest of them were so tall that little children could stand upright underneath. The place was as tangled and twisty as the densest forest, and here it was that a duck was sitting on her nest. It was time for her to hatch out her little ducklings, but it was such a long job that she was beginning to lose patience.

She hardly ever had a visitor; the other ducks thought more of swimming about in the moat than of coming and sitting under a dock-leaf just for the sake of a quack with her.

At last the eggs cracked open one after the other——"peep! peep!"——and all the yolks had come to life and were sticking out their heads.

"Quack, quack!" said the mother duck, and then the little ones scuttled out as quickly as they could, prying all round under the green leaves; and she let them do this as much as they liked, because green is so good for the eyes.

"Oh, how big the world is!" said the ducklings. And they certainly had much more room now than when they were lying in the egg.

"Do you suppose this is the whole world?" said their mother. "Why, it goes a long way past the other side of the garden, right into the parson's field; but I've never been as far as that. Well, you're all out now, I hope"——and she got up from her nest——"no, not all; the largest egg is still here. How ever long will it be? I can't bother about it much more." And she went on sitting again.

"Well, how's it going?" asked an old duck who came to pay a call.

"There's just this one egg that's taking such a time," said the sitting duck. "It simply won't break. But just look at the others—the loveliest ducklings I've ever seen. They all take after their father—the wretch! Why doesn't he come and see me?"

"Let's have a look at the egg which won't crack," said the old duck. "I'll bet it's a turkey's egg. That's how I was bamboozled

once. The little ones gave me no end of trouble, for they were afraid of the water—fancy that!—I just couldn't get them to go in. I quacked and clacked, but it was no good. Let's have a look at the egg. Ay, that's a turkey's egg, depend upon it! Let it be, and teach the others to swim."

"I think I'll sit just a little while yet," said the duck. "I've been sitting so long that it won't hurt to sit a little longer."

"Please yourself!" said the old duck, and away she waddled.

At last the big egg cracked. There was a "peep! peep!" from the young one as he tumbled out, looking so large and ugly. The duck glanced at him and said: "My! what a huge great duckling that is! None of the others look a bit like that. Still, it's never a turkey-chick, I'll be bound. Well, we shall soon find out. He shall go into the water, if I have to kick him in myself!"

The next day the weather was gloriously fine, with sun shining on all the green dock-leaves. The mother duck with her whole family came down to the moat. Splash! Into the water she jumped. "Quack, quack!" she said, and one after another the ducklings plomped in after her. The water closed over their heads, but they were up again in a moment and floated along so beautifully. Their legs worked of their own accord, and now the whole lot were in the water—even the ugly grey duckling joined in the swimming.

"It's no turkey, that's certain," said the duck. "Look how beautifully he uses his legs and how straight he holds himself. He's my own little one all right, and he's quite handsome, when you really come to look at him. Quack, quack! Now, come along

with me and let me show you the world and introduce you all
to the barnyard, but mind and keep close to me, so that nobody
steps on you; and keep a sharp lookout for the cat."

Then they made their way into the duckyard. There was a
fearful noise going on, for there were two families fighting for an
eel's head, and after all it was the cat that got it.

"You see! That's the way of the world," said the mother duck
and licked her bill, for she too had fancied the eel's head.
"Now then, where are your legs?" she said. "Look slippy and make
a nice bow to the old duck over there. She's the most genteel of
all these; she has Spanish blood, that's why she's so plump.
And do you see that crimson rag she wears on one leg?

It's extremely fine; it's the highest distinction any duck can win. It's as good as saying that there is no thought of getting rid of her; man and beast are to take notice! Look alive, and don't turn your toes in! A well-bred duckling turns its toes out, like father and mother — that's it. Now make a bow and say quack!"

They all obeyed; but the other ducks round about looked at them and said out loud: "There! Now we've got to have that rabble as well — as if there weren't enough of us already! Ugh! What a sight that duckling is! We can't possibly put up with

him"——and one duck immediately flew at him and bit him in the neck.

"Leave him alone," said the mother. "He's doing no one any harm."

"Yes, but he's so gawky and peculiar," said the one that had pecked him, "so he'll have to be squashed."

"What pretty children you have, my dear!" said the old duck with the rag on her leg. "All of them but one, who doesn't seem right. I only wish you could make him all over again."

"No question of that, my lady," said the ducklings' mother. "He's not pretty, but he's so good-tempered and he can swim just as well as the others—I daresay even a bit better. I fancy his looks will improve as he grows up, or maybe in time he'll grow down a little. He lay too long in the egg—that's why he isn't quite the right shape." And then she plucked his neck for him and smoothed out his feathers. "Anyhow, he's a drake, and so it doesn't matter so much," she added. "I feel sure he'll turn out pretty strong and be able to manage all right."

"The other ducklings are charming," said the old duck. "Make yourselves at home, my dears, and if you should find such a thing as an eel's head, you may bring it to me."

And so they made themselves at home.

But the poor duckling, who was the last out of the egg and looked so ugly, got pecked and jostled and teased by ducks and hens alike. "The great gawk!" they all clucked. And the turkey, who was born with spurs and therefore thought himself an emperor puffed up his feathers like a ship under full sail and went straight at him, and then he gobble-gobbled till he was quite red in the face. The poor duckling didn't know where to turn; he was terribly upset over being so ugly and the laughing stock of the whole barnyard.

That's how it was the first day, and afterwards things grew worse and worse. The poor duckling got chivied about by all of them; even his own brothers and sisters treated him badly, and they kept saying: "If only the cat would get you, you ridiculous great guy!" And the mother herself wished he were far away. The ducks nipped him, the hens pecked him and the maid who had to feed the poultry let fly at him with her foot.

After that, he ran away and fluttered over the hedge, and the little birds in the bushes grew frightened and flew into the air. "That's because I'm so ugly," thought the duckling and closed his eyes — and yet managed to get away. Eventually he came out to the great marsh where the wild ducks lived and lay there all night, utterly tired and dispirited.

In the morning the wild ducks flew up and looked at their new companion. "What ever are you?" they asked, and the duckling turned in every direction and bowed as well as he could.

"What a scarecrow you are!" said the wild ducks. "But that won't matter to us, as long as you don't marry into our family." Poor thing! He wasn't dreaming of getting married; all he wanted was to be allowed to stay quietly among the rushes and drink a little marsh water. After he had been there for two whole days, two wild geese came along—or rather two wild ganders, for they were both males. It was not long since they were hatched; that's why they were so perky.

"Look here, my lad!" they began. "You are so ugly that we quite like you. Will you come in with us and migrate? Not far off, in another marsh, are some very nice young wild geese, none of them married, who can quack beautifully. Here's a chance for you to make a hit, ugly as you are."

"Bang! Bang!" suddenly echoed above them, and both the ganders fell down dead in the rushes, and the water became red with blood. "Bang! Bang!" sounded once more, and flocks of wild geese flew up from the rushes, so that immediately, fresh shots rang out. A big shoot was on. The party lay ready all round the marsh; some even sat up in the trees on the branches that stretched right out over the rushes. Clouds of blue smoke drifted in among the dark trees and hung far over the water. Splashing through the

mud came the gun dogs, bending back reeds and rushes this way and that. It was terrifying for the poor duckling, who was just turning his head round to bury it under his wing, when he suddenly found close beside him a fearsome great dog with lolling tongue and grim, glittering eyes. It lowered its muzzle right down to the duckling, bared its sharp teeth and—splash!—it went off again without touching him.

The duckling gave a sigh of relief. "Thank goodness, I'm so ugly that even the dog doesn't fancy the taste of me." And he lay there quite still, while the shot pattered on the reeds and crack after crack was heard from the guns.

It was late in the day before everything was quiet again, but the poor duckling didn't dare to get up yet; he waited several hours longer before he took a look round and then made off from the marsh as fast as he could go. Over field and meadow he scuttled, but there was such a wind that he found it difficult to get along.

Towards evening he came up to a poor little farm cottage; it was so broken-down that it hardly knew which way to fall, and so it remained standing. The wind whizzed so fiercely round the duckling that he had to sit on his tail so as not to be blown over. The wind grew worse and worse. Then he noticed that the door had come off one of its hinges and hung so much on the slant that he could slip into the house through the crack. And that's just what he did.

There was an old woman living here with her cat and her hen. The cat, whom she called Sonny, could arch its back and purr; it could even give out sparks, if you stroked its fur the wrong way. The hen had such short little legs that it was called Chickabiddy Shortlegs; it was a very good layer, and the woman loved it like her own child.

Next morning they at once noticed the strange duckling, and the cat started to purr and the hen to cluck. "Why, what's up?" said the woman, looking round. But her sight wasn't very good, and she took the duckling for a fat duck that had lost its way. "My! What a find!" she said. "I shall be able to have duck's eggs—as long as it isn't a drake! We must give it a trial."

And so the duckling was taken on trial for three weeks; but there was no sign of an egg. Now, the cat was master in the house and the hen was mistress, and they always used to say, "We and the world," because they fancied that they made up half the world—what's more, much the superior half of it. The duckling thought there might be two opinions about that, but the hen wouldn't hear of it.

"Can you lay eggs?" she asked.

"No."

"Well, then, hold your tongue, will you!"

And the cat asked: "Can you arch your back or purr or give out sparks?"

"No."

"Well, then, your opinion's not wanted, when sensible people are talking."

And the duckling sat in the corner, quite out of spirits. Then suddenly he remembered the fresh air and the sunshine, and he got such a curious longing to swim in the water that—he couldn't help it—he had to tell the hen.

"What's the matter with you?" she asked. "You haven't anything to do—that's why you get these fancies. They'd soon go, if only you'd lay eggs or else purr."

"But it's so lovely to swim in the water," said the duckling, "so lovely to duck your head in it and dive down to the bottom."

"Most enjoyable, I'm sure," said the hen. "You must have gone crazy. Ask the cat about it—I've never met anyone as clever as he is—ask him if he's fond of swimming or diving! I say nothing of myself. Ask our old mistress, the wisest woman in the world! Do you suppose that she's keen on swimming and diving?"

"You don't understand me," said the duckling.

"Well, if we don't understand you, I should like to know who

would. Surely you'll never try and make out you are wiser than the cat and the mistress—not to mention myself. Don't be silly, child! Give thanks to your Maker for all the kindness you have met with. Haven't you come to a nice warm room where you have company that can teach you something? But you're just a stupid, and there's no fun in having you here. You may take my word for it—if I say unpleasant things to you, it's all for your good; that's just how you can tell which are your real friends. Only see that you lay eggs and learn how to purr or give out sparks!"

"I think I'll go out into the wide world," said the duckling.

"Yes, do," said the hen.

And so the duckling went off. He swam in the water; he dived

down; but no animal would have anything to do with him because of his ugliness.

Autumn now set in. The leaves in the wood turned yellow and brown, the wind seized them and whirled them about, while the sky above had a frosty look. The clouds hung heavy with hail and snow, and the raven who perched on the fence kept squawking, "ow! ow!" he felt so cold. The very thought of it gave you the shivers. Yes, the poor duckling was certainly having a bad time.

One evening, when there was a lovely sunset, a whole flock of large handsome birds appeared out of the bushes. The duckling had never seen such beautiful birds, all glittering white with long, graceful necks. They were swans. They gave the most extraordinary cry, spread out their magnificent long wings and

flew from this cold country away to warmer lands and open lakes.
They mounted high, high up into the air, and the ugly little
duckling felt so strange as he watched them. He turned round and
round in the water like a wheel and craned his neck in their
direction, letting out a cry so shrill and strange that it quite scared
even himself. Ah! He could never forget those beautiful, fortunate
birds; and directly they were lost to sight he dived right down

to the bottom and when he came up again, he was almost beside himself. He had no idea what the birds were called, nor where they were flying to, and yet they were dearer to him than any he had ever known; he didn't envy them in the least—how could he ever dream of such loveliness for himself? He would be quite satisfied, if only the ducks would just put up with him, poor gawky-looking creature!

What a cold winter it was! The duckling had to keep swimming about in the water to prevent it freezing right up. But every night the pool he was swimming in grew smaller and smaller; then the ice froze so hard that you could hear it creaking. The duckling had to keep his feet moving all the time to prevent the water from closing up. At last he grew faint with exhaustion and lay quite still and finally froze fast in the ice.

Early next morning he was seen by a peasant who went out and broke the ice with his wooden clog and carried the duckling home to his wife. And there they revived him.

The children wanted to play with him, but the duckling was afraid they meant mischief and fluttered in panic right up into the milkbowl, so that the milk slopped over into the room. The woman screamed out and clapped her hands in the air, and then he flew into the butter tub, and from there down into the flour bin, and out of it again. Dear, dear, he did look an object! The woman screamed at him and hit at him with the tongs, and the children tumbled over each other trying to catch him—how they laughed

and shouted! It was a good thing the door was open; the
duckling darted out into the bushes and sank down, dazed,
in the new-fallen snow.

But it would be far too dismal to describe all the want and misery
the duckling had to go through during that hard winter. He was

sheltering among the reeds on the marsh, when the sun began to get warm again and the larks to sing; beautiful spring had arrived.

Then all at once he tried his wings; the whir of them was louder than before, and they carried him swiftly away. Almost

before he realized it, he found himself in a big garden with apple trees in blossom and sweet-smelling lilac that dangled from long green boughs right over the winding stream. Oh, it was so lovely here in all the freshness of spring! And straight ahead, out of the thicket, came three beautiful white swans, ruffling their feathers and floating so lightly on the water. The duckling recognized the splendid creatures and was overcome with a strange feeling of melancholy.

"I will fly across to them, those royal birds! They will peck me to death for daring, ugly as I am, to go near them. Never mind! Better to be killed by them than be nipped by the ducks, pecked by the hens, kicked by the girl who minds the poultry, and suffer hardship in winter." And he flew out on to the water and swam

towards the beautiful swans. As they caught sight of him, they darted with ruffled feathers to meet him. "Yes, kill me, kill me!" cried the poor creature and bowed his head to the water, awaiting death. But what did he see there in the clear stream? It was a reflection of himself that he saw in front of him, but no longer a clumsy greyish bird, ugly and unattractive—no, he was himself a swan!

It doesn't matter about being born in a duckyard, as long as you are hatched from a swan's egg.

He felt positively glad at having gone through so much hardship and want; it helped him to appreciate all the happiness and beauty that were there to welcome him. And the three great swans swam round and round and stroked him with their beaks.

Some little children came into the garden and threw bread and grain into the water, and the smallest one called out: "There's a new swan!" and the other children joined in with shouts of delight: "Yes, there's a new swan!" And they clapped their hands and danced about and ran to fetch father and mother. Bits of bread and cake were thrown into the water, and everyone said, "The new one is the prettiest—so young and handsome!" And the old swans bowed before him.

This made him feel quite shy, and he tucked his head away under his wing——he himself hardly knew why. He was too, too happy, but not a bit proud, for a good heart is never proud. He thought of how he had been despised and persecuted, and now he heard everybody saying that he was the loveliest of all lovely birds. And the lilacs bowed their branches to him right down to the water, and the sunshine felt so warm and kindly. Then he ruffled his feathers, raised his slender neck and rejoiced from his heart: "I never dreamed of so much happiness, when I was the ugly duckling."